A BOY CALLED
DEWI

Steffan Lloyd   Illustrations by Brett Breckon

Pont

This story happened many years ago, not long after the last Roman soldier returned home from Britain.

Warlike tribes from Europe had already begun invading the rich lands of the south and east; but with its deep valleys and high mountains, Wales wasn't so easy to attack. There were no big towns or cities, just isolated farms and settlements.

But even without foreign attackers, life was hard for ordinary people. Food was sometimes scarce and children often fell sick and died. Local chiefs and princes argued and fought over land.

Not many names survive from those dangerous times, but one stands out. That name is Dewi Sant.

Families often have a tale to tell when a new baby arrives, but few stories are as strange as the one about Dewi. His mother's name was Non and she was the daughter of a Pembrokeshire nobleman called Cynyr.

When her baby was about to be born, Non was caught in the middle of a terrible storm on the clifftop at Caerfai. She was clinging to a rock when it was struck by a bolt of lightning. As the rock split in two, her baby was born, bathed in a sea of brilliant light.

Capel Non (or Non's Chapel) was built in honour of Dewi's mother, and the ruins can still be visited today.

Dewi's father, Sandde (or Sant), came from an important royal family. Sandde and his brother were sons of a warrior king called Ceredig who became ruler of Ceredigion.

In those days it was common for leaders to seize land and then to give it to their followers as a prize for their bravery in battle.

Ceredig's father was a powerful ruler, with a large kingdom in north Wales. He gave some of the southern lands to Ceredig, Dewi's grandfather, as a reward for defending the local people against Irish invaders.

Today that part of Wales is still known as Ceredigion.

Dewi grew up close to the wild beauty of the west Wales coast. He loved the pull of the wind and the cry of gulls as they circled and swooped.

Dewi was a kind and gentle boy, concerned for the creatures
he saw around him. Perhaps his strange clifftop birth made
him especially sensitive to nature.

In those days not all children were lucky enough to go to school.

Children from poor families worked long hours in the fields.

Dewi was one of the fortunate ones. He attended a monastery school, and was taught by the monks. Monasteries were important places of learning, almost like colleges or universities today. Monks studied and taught many different subjects, including mathematics, Latin, and Greek, as well as reading the Bible, praying, and going to services in the monastery church.

The head of the monastery, the Abbot, saw it as part of his job to encourage young boys to become novices or trainee monks. Dewi studied hard to become a monk.

ewi was a good pupil and quickly learned to read the books in the monastery library. The books were written not in Welsh or English, but in Latin and Greek. It wasn't until much later that the Bible was translated into Welsh.

Books in those days were very precious and had to be handled with great care. It would be another 900 years before William Caxton invented the printing press.

Books in Dewi's time had to be copied by hand and just a few copies have survived. Some monks spent all their working lives in the *scriptorium*. *Scriptorium* is a Latin word which means 'a place of writing'.

Learning to write was an important task in the monastery. It meant that fresh copies of the Bible could be made. Some of the monks worked as scribes, or copiers.

After the words had all been copied, the most important books were illustrated, sometimes with pictures, sometimes with beautifully decorated capital letters.

Pupils like Dewi first learned to write by using a pointed tool called a stylus. They pressed the stylus into a sheet of wax which could be smoothed out and used again and again.

When the trainee scribes got better at writing they were given a pen made from a goose feather, or cut from a reed.

Although Dewi enjoyed learning new things, he liked nothing better than to be out in the fresh air, enjoying the wild and wonderful scenery near his seaside home.

He liked being with his friends at the monastery school; he loved the company of the other children in the village; but sometimes he just needed to be alone.

He would run and play in the sunshine, shouting with joy as he raced the waves. Sometimes he sang hymns he'd learned at the monastery. Sometimes he made up songs of his own. Singing was the best way he knew of thanking God for a beautiful world.

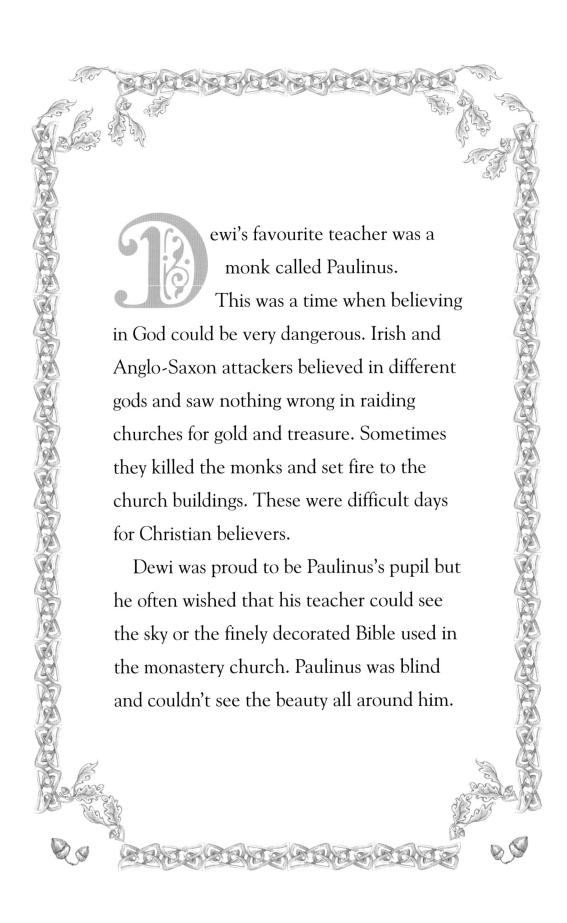

Dewi's favourite teacher was a monk called Paulinus.

This was a time when believing in God could be very dangerous. Irish and Anglo-Saxon attackers believed in different gods and saw nothing wrong in raiding churches for gold and treasure. Sometimes they killed the monks and set fire to the church buildings. These were difficult days for Christian believers.

Dewi was proud to be Paulinus's pupil but he often wished that his teacher could see the sky or the finely decorated Bible used in the monastery church. Paulinus was blind and couldn't see the beauty all around him.

ecause of his blindness, Paulinus had to rely on other people. It was easier for him in the monastery because he knew where everything was. Outside, in unfamiliar places, it was much harder.

The monks believed it was their duty to teach people about Jesus; they would sometimes travel long distances to remote villages. There were no proper roads in those days and Paulinus always needed someone to guide him over rough ground. He was glad of a young and willing helper like Dewi.

As Dewi grew older he wished very much that he could help his teacher to regain his sight. He prayed very hard that God would show him how.

In the cool stillness of the evening,
Dewi would sit quietly in the
monastery church, thinking about
Paulinus and his blindness.

Suddenly he realised what he needed
to do.

Dewi waited until morning, then went to find
his teacher.

'Trust me,' he said, laying one hand on
Paulinus's shoulder and the other across
his eyes.

'No,' said the old man gently. 'I put my
trust in God alone.'

For a moment, Paulinus was afraid to open his eyes. Although his faith was strong, he could hardly believe that he would be able to see once more.

But when he stepped outside, the sudden brightness was almost too much for him. The light was dazzling. Then, as he got used to the sunshine, he started to see the things he'd missed for so many years.

The world was even more beautiful than he remembered. The sky was bluer, the hills were greener, and tiny scraps of colour glowed like jewels.

He could even see the woven threads in the coarse brown fabric of his habit.

As he gazed in wonder, Paulinus remembered to say thank you to God.

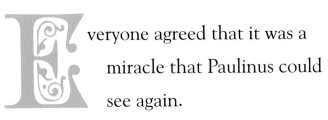

Everyone agreed that it was a miracle that Paulinus could see again.

It wasn't the first miracle in Dewi's young life and it certainly wouldn't be the last.

When he grew up, Dewi became an important bishop and built a monastery at St Davids. Today it is the home of a cathedral which children visit when they come to Pembrokeshire on holiday.

Dewi, or Saint David as he is often known, would have been so pleased to meet them!

'Do the little things in life.'

'Gwnewch y pethau bychain.'

Dewi Sant, patron saint of Wales

Published in Wales in 2010 by Pont Books, an imprint of
Gomer Press, Llandysul, Ceredigion, SA44 4JL

ISBN 978 1 84851 153 8

A CIP record for this title is available from the British Library.

This book is published with the financial support of the
Welsh Books Council.

Printed and bound in Wales at Gomer Press,
Llandysul, Ceredigion